The Magic Helmet
A Viking Adventure

D0928480

00636095

'The Magic Helmet: A Viking Adventure'
An original concept by Cath Jones
© Cath Jones

Illustrated by Dean Gray

Published by MAVERICK ARTS PUBLISHING LTD

Studio 3A, City Business Centre, 6 Brighton Road,

Horsham, West Sussex, RH13 5BB

© Maverick Arts Publishing Limited November 2018

+44 (0)1403 256941

A CIP catalogue record for this book is available at the British Library.

ISBN 978-1-84886-390-3

www.maverickbooks.co.uk

Waltham Forest Libraries	
904 000 00636095	
Askews & Holts	21-Dec-2018
NEW	£5.99
5923470	

This book is rated as: White Band (Guided Reading)

The Magic Helmet
A Viking Adventure

By Cath Jones

Illustrated by Dean Gray

Chapter 1

"Have fun!" Mum called. "I'll be back in two weeks." Then she drove off.

Harry stared round the living room. How would he survive two whole weeks with Gran? There was no internet and no computer. He couldn't even go outside to explore because it was raining!

Gran pointed at a record player. "Why don't you play some of Grandad's records until the

rain stops?"

A photograph stood next to the record player.
Harry looked at it curiously. It showed Grandad
with his enormous red
beard, holding a Viking
helmet.

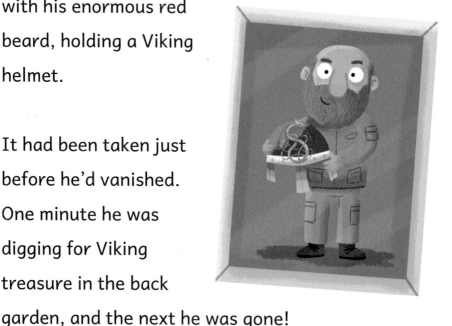

It had been taken just
before he'd vanished.
One minute he was
digging for Viking
treasure in the back
garden, and the next he was gone!

Harry wished he could ask Gran about how
Grandad disappeared, but Mum had made him

promise not to.

He sighed and pressed a button on the record player. A record began to spin round.

"*Old Norse* for beginners," said a crackly voice.

"Grandad used that record to learn Old Norse," said Gran. "It's the language the Vikings spoke."

"Lesson one - Skip – Biti – Kot," said the crackly voice.

Harry repeated the Viking words. "Skip – Biti – Kot." To his surprise, it was fun!

An hour later, the rain finally stopped.

"Yeah!" Harry sprinted into the garden.
He kicked a stone high into the air.

CLANK!

What had he hit?

The rain had washed away a lot of soil and
something was sticking out of the ground.
His heart leapt with excitement.

He began to dig with his hands. Finally, he
pulled something free of the mud. He gasped.
It was a helmet! It was decorated with a
curling dragon.

Harry put it on his head. Suddenly, there was a loud bang like a clap of thunder.

The helmet slid down over his eyes and –

WHOOSH!

Chapter 2

Harry landed on his bottom. He pulled off the helmet and gazed around in shock. Gran's garden had vanished. He was sitting in a boat next to a large dog. At the front of the boat was a wooden, snarling dragon's head. It looked like a Viking longboat!

Was the helmet a time travel helmet?

Had he travelled over one thousand years back in time? Had the same thing happened to Grandad?

Harry closed his eyes and opened them again. He was still on the boat. The dog licked his hand.

"Have you seen my Grandad?" Harry whispered. The dog didn't reply.

Harry peeped over the side of the boat. The cold sea-wind felt lovely on his face. Three more longboats were speeding along close by. In the distance, Harry spotted land.

Drops of rain began to fall. The Vikings lowered

the big square sail. They put it over the boat like a tent. Then they poked oars through holes in the side of the boat. They began to row. The longboat oars dipped in and out of the water with a quiet swish-swish-swish.

Harry snuggled close to the dog to keep warm. "I wonder where we're going?" he murmured.

Suddenly there was a loud shout. "I am Harald the Brave," said an enormous and rather scary looking Viking. "This is *my* ship and I don't like stowaways, especially weirdly dressed ones like you!"

Harry listened in surprise. He could understand what they were saying! Then he began to shake

with fear. Grandad had told him all about the Vikings. They were sea-pirates known for theft, trickery and murder!

"Please let me stay," he begged.

"If you want to stay on this boat, you must work," Harald the Brave snarled. "You can look after Wolf, our leader's dog, but you don't need a helmet for that." He snatched Harry's helmet and took it away.

"Oh no!" thought Harry. "I need that helmet to get home!"

Chapter 3

The longboat was heading up a river. The Vikings rowed in silence but Harry could tell they were excited.

Harald the Brave let out a sinister laugh and handed Harry a big wooden stick. "You might need this later, to defend yourself!"

Harry swung it like a sword. He felt like a Viking warrior!

"We will call you Stick Swinger," Harald the Brave said in a gruff voice.

As soon as the bright sun went behind a cloud, the Vikings landed their boats. First, they threw a spear into the water.

"A gift to the god Thor!" said Harald the Brave.

Everyone wrapped sheepskin around their feet. Then they leapt from the longboat. They crept silently along the shore. Harry followed, keeping Wolf close to his side.

Soon they came to a village.

"Stay at the back," Harald the Brave ordered Harry.

"Where are all the people?" Harry whispered.

"They are hiding in their huts!" Harald the Brave laughed.

Harald the Brave pointed at a large building with a thatched roof. "That's where we'll find their treasure," he said. "You and Wolf keep

watch." He broke down the door with his axe.

"I'm sure Grandad must be here somewhere," Harry whispered to Wolf. "Let's find him!"

They crept between the small huts and looked for clues. Soon, loud shouts and the sound of fighting could be heard coming from the big building.

What if someone comes out and spots us? thought Harry nervously. He gripped his stick tightly.

Finally, the noise seemed to quieten, until Harry heard Harald shout:

"Back to the boat!"

The Vikings carried away chests filled with coins and treasure. They stole animals and food too.

"It was a hard fight but tonight we will celebrate our victory with a feast!" said Harald the Brave.

Harry sighed with disappointment. They had found no sign of Grandad anywhere.

Chapter 4

After the raid, the Vikings started to dig an enormous hole close to the river.

Harry watched in surprise as they put one of the longboats in the hole. Then they filled the boat with things: cooking pots and swords and helmets. Finally, the body of a Viking warrior was placed in the boat.

Harald the Brave saw Harry's puzzled expression. "He died bravely, but now he must go to Valhalla, the great hall of the gods. He will need all these things in his next life."

Harry and Wolf helped the warriors bury the boat. Then they gathered up large stones and placed them round it. When all the stones were used up, Harry realised he could see the outline of the boat.

Suddenly, three blasts of a war horn sounded.

Harald the Brave leapt up. "At last, our leader has returned."

Two longboats glided out of the mist. A Viking was standing on the first boat. He threw two spears into the waves.

Harry stared. There was something different about this Viking. He wore a tunic and belt and carried a round shield and a battle axe, but there was no sign of his helmet. He was also shorter than the others and had the bushiest and reddest beard.

The new arrival jumped off the boat and sank deep into the soft ground. The weight of the weapons was too much. Behind the bushy orange beard, a smile twitched.

Wolf whimpered. Suddenly, he broke free and charged up to the man. The Viking bent down and Wolf licked his face.

Harry gasped in sudden realisation. He ran down the beach and threw his arms around the Viking. The Viking looked down in surprise – but then he suddenly turned and hugged Harry tight.

Grandad was the Viking leader!

Chapter 5

"Harry!" gasped Grandad. His eyes shone with delight. "What are you doing here?"

"It's a long story! I found a Viking helmet and it brought me here," Harry laughed. "Everyone misses you so much."

A far-away look came into

Grandad's eyes and he nodded. "Perhaps it is time for my Viking adventure to come to an end."

Suddenly, Harald the Brave appeared at their side. "You know each other?" he said in surprise.

Grandad smiled and nodded.

"It's good to have you back Eric Redbeard," Harald the Brave said. "You arrive in time to feast."

The Vikings roasted a pig and gathered to listen to stories. They passed round a helmet filled with a sweet smelling liquid and took sips.

Harry was surprised to find it tasted like honey.

While Harald the Brave told stories of great
Viking warriors and adventures, Grandad
explained everything that had happened: how
he'd found the helmet in the back garden, had
tried it on and **WHOOSH!** It had brought him
here! However, he'd lost his magical helmet
when his longboat sunk.

"Harald the Brave took my helmet," Harry said.

Grandad gave Harry's arm a squeeze. "Don't worry, I'll get it back."

Harry watched as Grandad went and talked with Harald. A few minutes later, Grandad returned with a sack.

"Harald the Brave said you earned this for doing such a good job looking after Wolf," Grandad said.

Harry peered into the sack. "My helmet!" He grabbed Grandad's hand and put on the helmet. "Hold on tight!"

There was a loud clap of thunder. Wolf yelped in surprise and leapt into Grandad's arms –

WHOOSH!

Grandad, Harry and Wolf landed in the middle of the garden back home. Gran came running out of the house.

"Eric! Where on earth have you been?" Gran said, throwing her arms around him.

"Sorry to have been so long." Grandad winked at Harry. "I got a little lost..."

The End

Book Bands for Guided Reading

The Institute of Education book banding system is a scale of colours that reflects the various levels of reading difficulty. The bands are assigned by taking into account the content, the language style, the layout and phonics. Word, phrase and sentence level work is also taken into consideration.

Maverick Early Readers are a bright, attractive range of books covering the pink to white bands. All of these books have been book banded for guided reading to the industry standard and edited by a leading educational consultant.

Pink
Red
Yellow
Blue
Green
Orange
Turquoise
Purple
Gold
White

To view the whole Maverick Readers scheme, visit our website at

www.maverickearlyreaders.com

Or scan the QR code above to view our scheme instantly!